ACKNOWLEDGMENTS

I'd like to thank the following folks for their expert help:

Layout & Text Design: Jessie Horsting
Lettering: Carrie Spiegle
Coloring: Joe Chiodo with assists from: Bruce Timm, Brent Anderson, Scott Saavedra, Jennifer Frank
General Troubleshooting: Bob Chapman
Inspiration & Advice: Doug Wildey, Bill Stout, Rich Hescox, John Koukoutsakis, Mark Evanier, & "Jeffty" Ellison.

Special Thanks to "Hurricane" Jaime Hernandez for a last minute art assist.

The Rocketeer TM 1985 Dave Stevens. Entire contents copyright © Dave Stevens. Introduction copyright © 1985 by the Kilimanjaro Corporation. All rights reserved. No portion of this book may be reprinted or reproduced without the express permission of the author or the author's agent. © 1985

ISBN 0-913035-06-8 Paperback by Eclipse Books
ISBN 0-913035-05- X Hardcover Edition by Graphitti Designs

Photo Credits: History of Aviation Collection
Vince Davis Aeronautical Archives

Printed in the U.S.A.

THE ROCKETEER

AN ALBUM

DAVE STEVENS

· ECLIPSE BOOKS ·

DEDICATION

To my mom and pop:
Thanks for not giving me to the Gypsies.

THE ROCKETEER
INTRODUCTION
BY HARLAN ELLISON

Of all the possible who might have been solicited to jot down a few introductory notes to this Rocketeer graphic album, Dave Stevens selected me for a specific reason. An anecdote that happened eleven minutes ago (as I sit writing this on Saturday evening, March 30th 1985) captures that reason.

Dave came in with the first twelve pages of the material. The originals, reworked. He brought them along, I presume, to refresh my memory. He need not have bothered. I have all the Pacific Comics magazines that introduced The Rocketeer back in 1982. More, I remember them clearly. Memory is a large part of The Rocketeer. Memories of things that happened long before Dave was born, things that happened in 1938. I was four years old in 1938. Dave Stevens wouldn't be born for seventeen years yet. But he remembers.

So I reread those original twelve pages of The Rocketeer's first flight, as Dave watched. Didn't need to, but I did it. Then I walked across the room to my typewriter, here in my office, about eleven minutes ago, and I prepared to sit down and write many lines of glowing admiration for Dave's artwork and the special treasure that The Rocketeer has become for anybody who enjoys comics.

I work to music. Write to it; always have. So I pulled out a special tape cassette and dropped it into the carriage of the Bang & Olufsen. It was music specially selected for the mood of what I was about to write, music from the period of The Rocketeer. Some years ago an aficionado of swing music from the Twenties through the Forties, Les Zeiger, struck a deal with Dave Goldin of Radio Yesteryear, and they issued a series of more than forty "Z tapes" anthologizing obscure and wonderful music from those years. The tape I pulled and put on is titled "1927 - 1928 According to Victor" and it is noise-free repressings of the Victor Records catalogue from that period.

I said nothing to Dave. I just slipped the cassette into the carriage, hit the play touchplate, and as I sat down at the typewriter eleven minutes ago, the huge Quad Electrostatic Screens here in the office began to emit the sound of Victor 20791, recorded on February 28th, 1927 . . . three years more than a quarter of a century before Dave Stevens would be born, fifty-four years before Dave Stevens would draw his first tentative line of The Rocketeer.

"That's Jesse Crawford," Dave said, as the first four bars of *At Sundown* on the Wurlitzer resonated through my office.

I had been sitting down. I hadn't yet actually planted my butt and knees on the Balens Chair. I was so amazed, so utterly dumbfounded, so electrified by his recognition of one of the more obscure artists of the Twenties, that I stopped in mid-movement, felt the muscles of my jaw crack as my mouth dropped open, hung there half bent, spun, and stared at him. "My

*AP wire photo, April 12th, 1938
Chaplin Airfield, Los Angeles'
first look at the Rocketeer*

God," I said, in awe, "it *is* Jesse Crawford! How the hoot did you know that?"

Stevens did his patented disingenuous toe-scuffle, making as if there was nothing remarkable about a twenty-nine-year-old kid brought up on rock and (maybe, if he was sentient enough back then) a little doo-wop, recognizing a forgotten organist from four bars. Four puny bars!

But what happened over here eleven minutes ago is the codified example of why Dave asked me, of all possible, to write this introduction. I couldn't have ordered up a better touchstone if I'd programmed it.

Because, you see, I'm the one introducing The Rocketeer because about the time this book hits the printing press I'll be fifty-one years old, and I *grew up* with guys like Cliff Secord and his alter ego, The Rocketeer. I came to crave danger and adventure in my personal life because I was closer to The Green Hornet and The Shadow and Doc Savage and The Spider and Hop Harrigan than I was to Leon Miller or Johnny Mummy or even Joe Tobul and the rest of the kids at Lathrop Grade School.

And for those of you who remember only as far back as Silver Surfer and The Eagles, let me assure you that Dave Stevens *remembers* the period of The Rocketeer accurately. Don't ask how. Reincarnation is flummery. He just *knows*. The name Jesse Crawford doesn't simply pop onto someone's palate unbidden.

The story of The Rocketeer is filled with those accuracies. *You* don't need to recognize them, it's enough that Dave does. Because that's the true essence of *hommage*. Not that self-indulgent smart-alecky thing that Spielberg and his clone-children do in their films, filling every corner of the frame with little in-jokes and blatant references to the sci-fi crap that impressed them when they were ten years old, so distracting that you aren't supposed to notice that the movie center-screen is full of holes and has an empty soul.

Uh-uh. Stevens uses that stuff only to inform the telling of his story. Sure, I can look at Cliff Secord's girl friend Betty (which ought to be spelled Bette) and smile (while you only leer), because Dave has used as the model for female pulchritude the queen of the 1950's girlie magazines (for which I was writing and editing), the luscious Bette Page, high priestess of nylons, garter belts and spike heels. You don't need to know that Betty has the face of Bette (with the body of Dave's former wife, Charlene Brinke Stevens). She is a stunner, not only because Dave can draw women with such sauciness that they make Corben's casaba-breasted maidens and Frazetta's battleship-bottomed bimbos look like mutants, but because the shadow of Bette Page lives in those lines. You need never have read an issue of *Doc Savage*, need not recognize the apelike character who chums around with the natty dude in monocle and homburg, to get the sense that whatever little Dave cares to tell us about them, they (and their boss) are fully realized characters. And why the hell shouldn't they be fully formed? They already populate more than one hundred and eighty novels written under the pseudonym Kenneth Robeson. It don't matter nowhichway that you have never been to Cleveland in the Forties (where and when I grew up) to attend the Bendix air races, to enjoy a Powder Puff Derby, to recognize Secord's plane as being the famous, feisty little Gee Bee (Model Z). Don't matter nowhichway. Look at that nifty racer, the way it sings through Stevens's panels.

Actually, I feel sorry for most of you young farts. You can enjoy the dickens out of The Rocketeer, but insufficient years lie behind your eyelids to catch all the swell subtleties that Dave Stevens has lying quietly in the work. But because I remember, because Stevens just asked me if the version of "Just a Gigolo" that's playing is the Bing Crosby rendition (no, Dave, it's Ben Bernie and his Hotel Roosevelt Orchestra, 1931), because my favorite comic books are still the Canadian-produced *Grand Slam* and *Three Aces* (copies of which I'd dearly love to have after forty years), because there's a ten-year-old kid in me and a sixty-year-old codger in Stevens . . . that's the reason I was asked to write this introduction.

The Rocketeer is something special. For all the hopeful attempts at doing a period comic book that have popped up these last few years, popped and vanished, only The Rocketeer captures the feel of those days. The artwork is modern, yet it has a tone of the Twenties and Thirties. The dialogue isn't 100% of the times, but it's damned close. And even if the first two sections aren't as masterful as the final three—indicating that Stevens learned on the job—they are hip-deep in the right kind of nostalgia. They are adventure and affection, melded in just the right way to avoid the sickness of wishing for the past; they bring into the Eighties the richness of those wild times when we believed a man could fly, if only he had a rocket pack.

I was asked to write this intro, and you are lining up to buy this book, because deep in the marrow of even those of you who only know music as the fornicating-cricket sound of heavymetal, there is the sound of a big swing band playing *I'll Get By* for an audience of men with patent-leather hair and flappers wearing headache bands in a posh hotel ballroom.

Dave Stevens and his work somehow cross the boundaries of the dead years. And that's why, folks, that's why.

— HARLAN ELLISON
30 March 85
Los Angeles

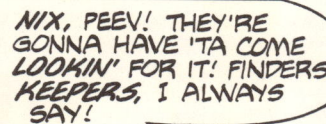

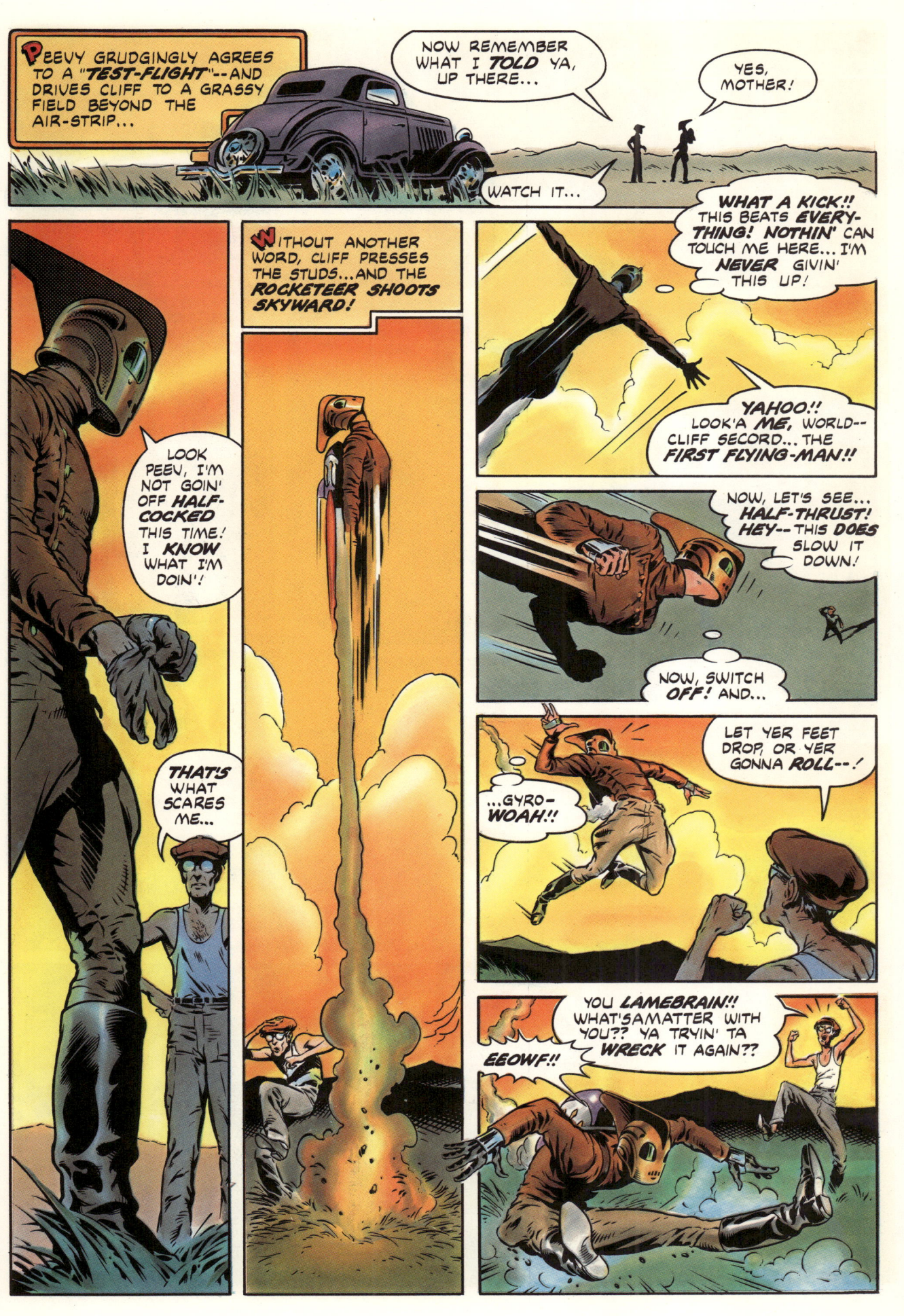

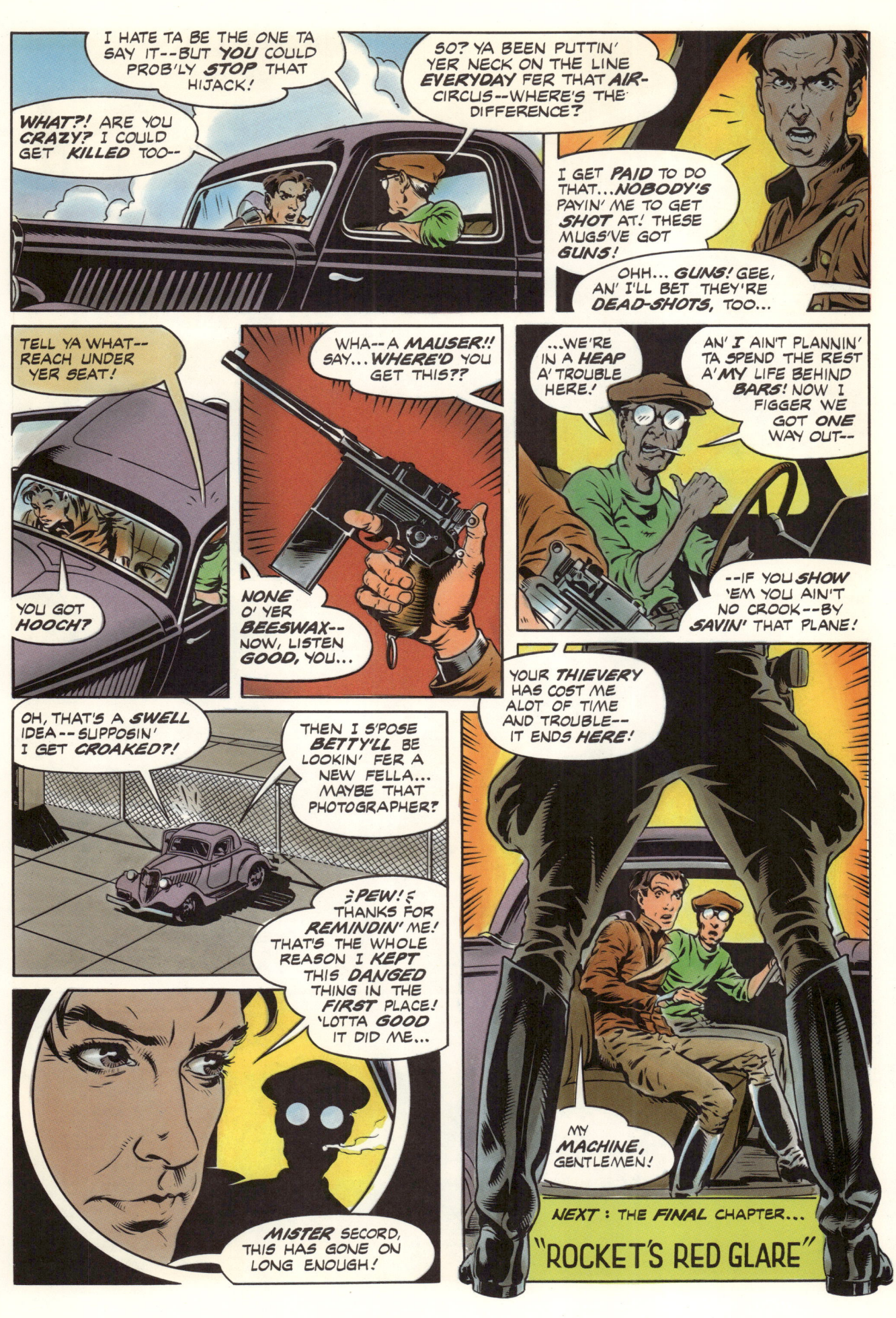

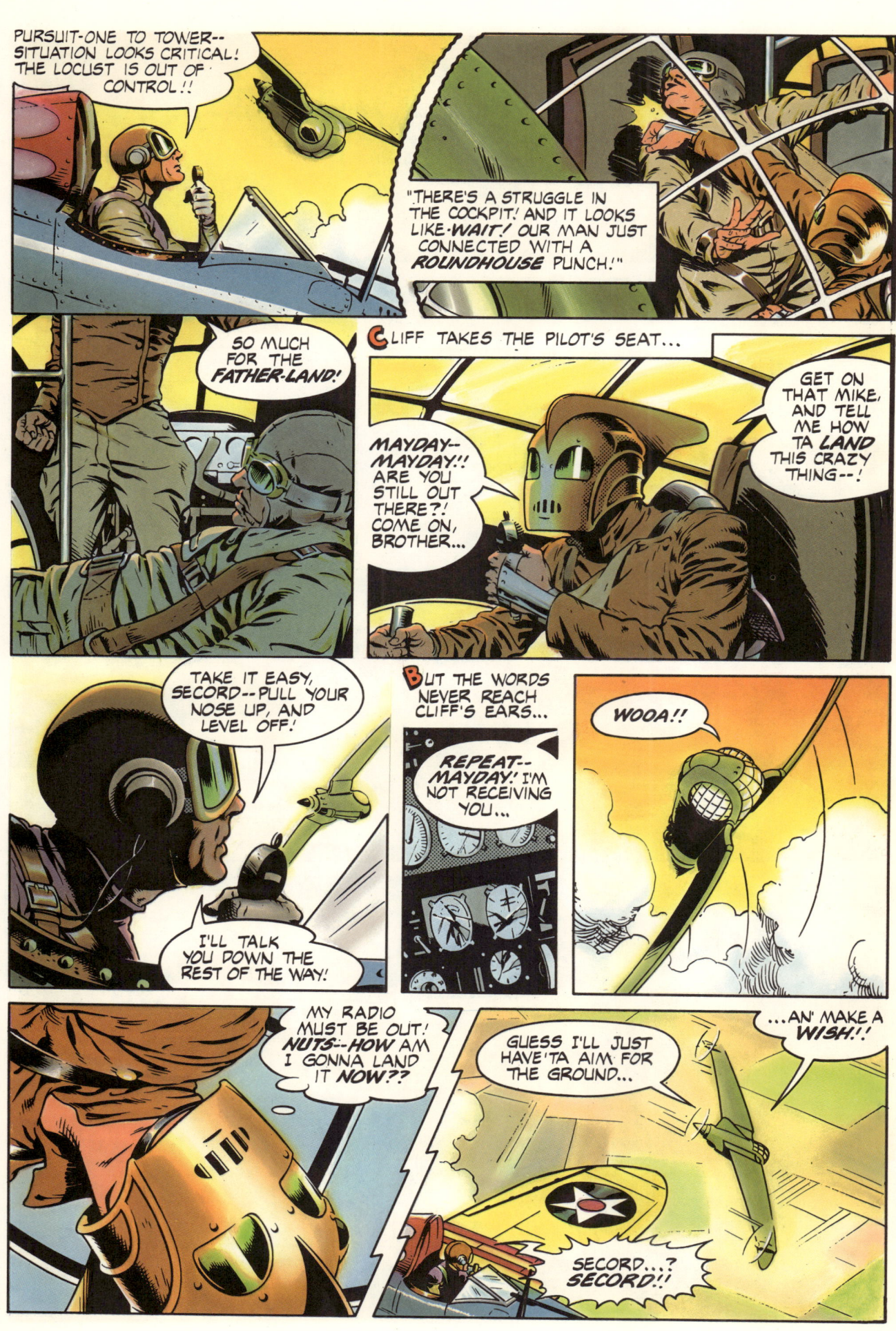

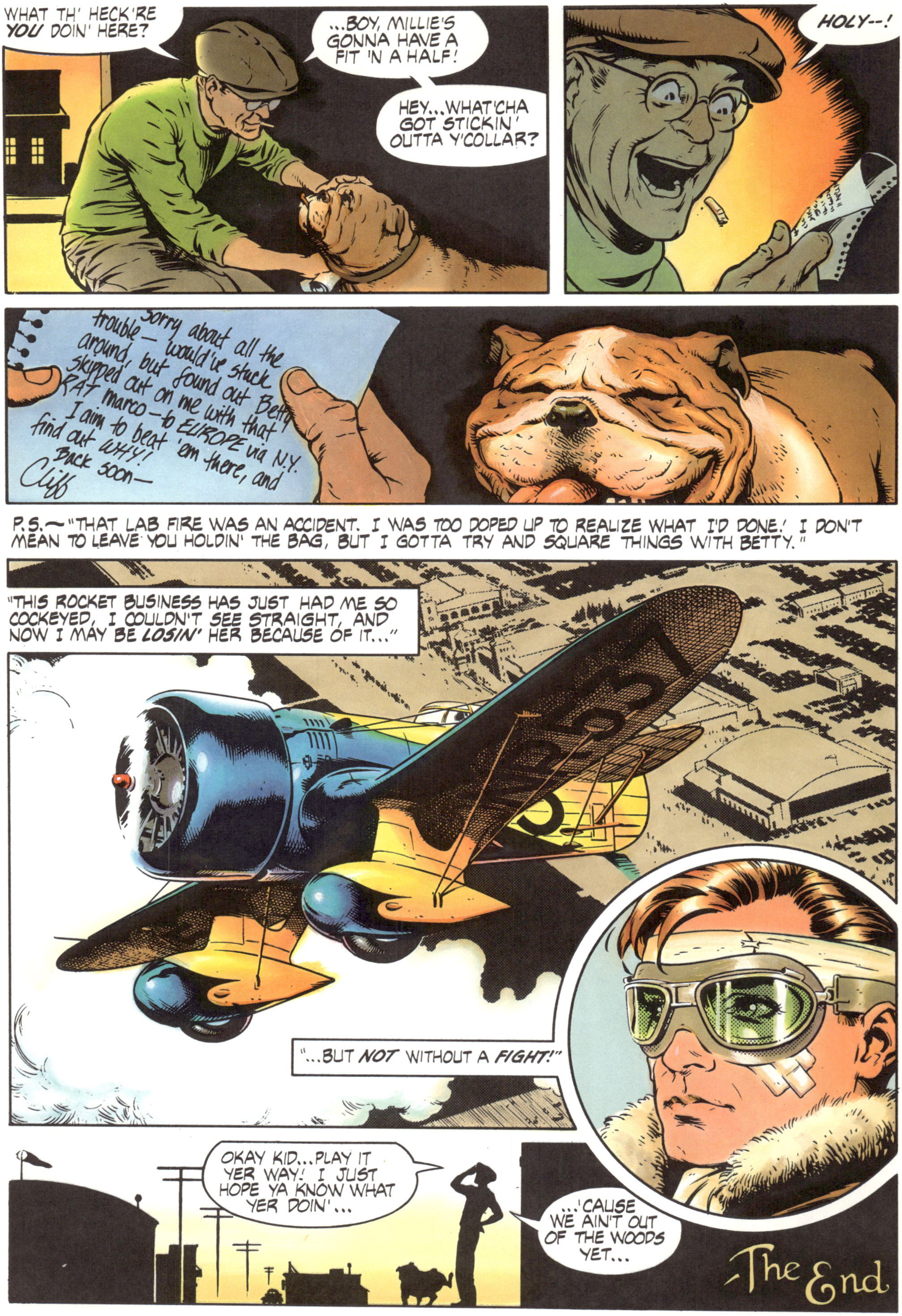